Daven's Return: the Wrath of God

Donald G Hunter

authorHOUSE®

AuthorHouse™
1663 Liberty Drive, Suite 200
Bloomington, IN 47403
www.authorhouse.com
Phone: 1-800-839-8640

First published by AuthorHouse 3/16/2009

ISBN: 978-1-4389-5401-1 (sc)

Printed in the United States of America
Bloomington, Indiana

This book is printed on acid-free paper.

Draven's Return: The Wrath of God

As a new day dawns with it brings forth new sins drugs, pollution, social and economic problems, the differences between the poor, and the rich. Abortion and the pedophile mixes with seven deadly sins, bringing forth change and weakens the gray line that protects man it upsets the balance of life in which man lives, the sins of men use to only happen at night, but now it happens at any time and any place in this world. Satin is upon us now and with him is a child who is now a man named Daven, Satins demons dig through the frozen ice of Antarctic behind them they pull a glass coffin made of diamonds, with a precious gift for their lord, Satin. As they cross over the gray line into Satins realm, his heat melts the ice as Satin removes the curse that mother nature, father time, and the grim reaper placed upon him as he slept Daven awake said Satin, for it is our time rise up out of hell and rule mother earth on heaven as well. For God will bow at our feet, as we rule his kingdom as father and son.

As Daven awakes free from the curse of sleep that the grim reaper has placed upon him, and being animated in time by father time. Yet the curse of mother nature remains upon him he opens his eyes but he cannot see, his mind has not cleared he moves but he cannot speak for his inner body is still frozen he finds himself in hells realm and the voice he can only hear is Satins,

Look what God has done to you my son, side with me and I will release the curse of mother nature, deny me and in this diamond glass coffin you will stay, for all eternity. For God did not wish you to be, there can only be one God, for that is he. Side with mankind and me my son and mother earth will be yours to do what you please.

All I wish is for heaven and hell to be one for me to rule. For I know the death of your mother, brother David and his wife Doris has brought you such grief, but in time they would have grown to betray you, and despise you for what you truly are. Just as God has. Can you see Daven; my love is the only true love you need. For I would never doubt you, or betray for my faith lies within thee.

The power you possess combined with mine will make us unstoppable. The universe and all that come with it could be ours for all eternity. With every word and syllable Satin gives his best to influence the child, to join as father and son to plague the world and to be against God and his beliefs.

Daven said Satin blink your eyes once for no to stay this way for all eternity or twice to release you. So you may walk the earth and get your revenge against God, Daven paused for a moment and then blinked twice. Then so be it Satin said

Satin slit his wrist and from his wrist Daven drinks Satins blood, warming him breaking the curse that mother nature has placed upon him. As he drinks his eyes turn from the soft brown to a fiery red for Satin has many of sins, against him making Daven more powerful and greater than before. Now said Satin you are of flesh of my flesh blood of my blood, my first born my demon son. Now rise up out of that coffin in which was your punishment that in prisoned you, and greet your newfound family the demon of hell.

Chapter Two: To All My Demons Satin Speaks

The promise I have made to you is upon us now meet my new first born son, Lord Daven for hell and heaven will be as one to rule and the demons cheer to there lord Satin and his first born son, for several years Daven remained inside the darkness of hell he requests to Satin, to go to mother earth. To walk the earth again father it will do me some good yes my son said Satin you have been here for years inside hells darkness, so it will be forbidden for you to walk in mother earths sunlight, the evening dust before dark will the best time to go. Be back before dawn for the sun will blind your eyes and blister your skin. Yes my lord father Satin. Daven take with you four demons to protect you my son. For if God finds out you exist again he will not be merciful to you, but will rid of you by death if he could. Said Satin I will be careful my lord and return before dawn. So be it said Satin you may go.

When Daven returns to mother earth he spends most of his time visiting the lake were his mother Heidi, brother David, and his wife Doris were layed to rest. As Daven walks upon the farm he kneels to his knees to feel the earth beneath him the soil felt dry and brittle and some spots were hard like clay. So he blessed the ground and changed the climate back to the way he had it in the past as he came up to the barn to check the animals Joes dog started to bark furoscisly, a voice cries out its Joe shut up you dam mutt, were trying to sleep John comes to the front door Joe he said, there's someone out there they are standing by the barn.

Get the gun said Joe, and wake up Stevo, John. Betty Johns wife is waken by the barking dog Betty get Stevo said John, Stevo wake up said Betty someone is trying to steal one or more of the animals, out of the barn Stevo jumps up and out the bed and runs to the front door.ssh Stevo there's five of them one is in the barn John whispers as he and Stevo slowly walks off the porch John asks Stevo were your gun? In the house he said what good is it in the house. Said John find something.

Stevo grabs a two by four as they creep around the side of the barn staying out of the moonlight so they cannot be seen, they sneak inside the barn, through the side door. As Stevo raises the two by four John aims his gun, the four demons of hell grabs them both Daven then turns around John and Stevo it is I. John and Stevo speak Daven it is you? Yes John and Stevo it is I. Release them at once and wait for me inside the shadows of the darkness, yes my lord Daven. The demons said. Daven come inside said John speak with father Joe for he would love to hear from you, and meet my lovely wife,

I could only stay for a little while for it will be morning soon, said Daven. Then just to say hello said Stevo for we will always be your family, Daven.and you will always be welcome here. That is why I have returned said Daven. For I belong here with my true family. Inside the house Daven speaks to farmer Joe and meets his brother Johns lovely wife.theres more said John he opened the door were Davens bedroom use to be were he had studied day and night about God, look inside Daven, laying in two separate beds are two young boys, these are my sons one is named David and the other is named after you Daven. The two little brothers are beautiful just as we are. I must go now the sun is rising, but I will return when the dust fill the sky it would be about dinnertime; I will meet your boys then. As Daven walks away with his four demons, from hell they disappear as they walk through the field. Betty could not believe her eyes as she stevo, and her husband John wave to him. Saying we will see you soon, John she asks who is Daven? He is our brother who has a special gift. You to will come to love him as we do. I promise you that so don't be afraid of our brother Daven promise me. Yes John I promise said Betty. As Daven kept his promise to John he returned at dust with his four demons of hell. Who wait for Daven in the shadow of the night, to protect him if need so.

With Daven out of the way Satin plans his attack on mother earth. He speaks to his warriors of demons, the time is near as soon as the child Daven performs a miracle upon mother earth, it will weaken the gray line even more. Making it easy for us to cross, and to plague mother earth.

With our soldiers of demons in large numbers, upsetting the balance of good verse evil, bringing God down from the heavens to wage war upon mother earth, to save mankind, we must seize and hold the gray line and never surrender it, but push the fight up to the heaven and finish it there. Were heaven and hell will become as one. For I Satin to rule.

My lord what about Daven? All he wants is mother earth; he will be satisfied with just that. My lord do not under estimate him. Even though your blood controls his every being, he will find a way to free himself and seek the truth. As the demons of hell chant and hail their lord Satin, the lead demon knows he speaks the truth so he walks upon mother earth to keep an eye on Daven, for there is no return from the death of a demon.

For when a demon dies, it can never return it just leaves an opportunity for a stronger demon to break through, and bring new sins and inhabit with in mans flesh, torturing and punishing his soul to fight to own ones spirit. To claim as his own to posses, home again

As Daven and John speaks, he meets his nephews for the first time, John your children are so behaved, and well mannered. Mother would be proud of you. The children that come to me are damned, for they lost respect for their parents and others as well. They over dose on drugs are committing suicide and murdering by joining gangs, only to feel that they belong. What a waste of life all they do is cry out for attention and there for the quality time and love they did not receive upon mother earth so

They run amuck only to be damned did you know John the next best thing to God is that of a women for she carries the seeds that bare the fruit of life if she is absent the fruit becomes sour and the child develops disobedience it acts out crying for attention so it is wrong and forgets what is right, all because it has lost faith and trust in her.

So he wishes her dead to do what it pleases without being controlled by her, the child becomes lost within a world of its own anger as they sit down for dinner they bless the food they eat, at this time the lead demon curses the food and a large piece of meat gets enlarged in little Daven, throat Betty screams to John your son Daven is choking, no matter how hard John tried he could not release it from his throat, he was suffocating and his face turned a grayish blue and his body went limp, is he dead asked Betty I believe so said John. Then Daven spoke bring the child before me.

Daven then reached into the child's mouth and removed the meat. That was enlarged in his throat. Then he blessed the child with the breath of life, he's coming to welcome back little one said Daven. By Daven performing this miracle it weakened the gray line a great deal. The lead demon returned to Satins den, the deed is done I have made your son Daven use his gift to perform a miracle upon mother earth. Now we may cross over and take what is ours, and begin the war that would end all wars. For there will be no difference just demons upon demons, with one ruler Satin as God, All else will be enslaved and imprisoned and the women would bare children in Satins image. And for man if he don't pledge his soul onto Satin he will be put to death for heaven and hell would be converted into one realm, so Satin walked to the gray line and strummed it with his finger and it vibrated like a loose cord. Then he passed his hand through the gray line he felt a tingle of earths gentle breeze so he crossed over and with him came his darkness his eyes did not go blind, and his flesh did not blister by the sun of mother earth.

At last Satin heaven and all that comes with it will soon be mine, and Satin laughed a laugh so hard that it sounded like thunder Daven looks to the horizon he noticed the sun rising early much early there is something wrong said Daven. When Satin crossed over he upset the balance of time, John I must go said Daven, is that the sun said Betty, we just had dinner not even an hour a go were did time go? Its morning already said Stevo my head had just hit the pillow. The family just looked out the window wondering why. John I must go said Daven. as Daven walked out the front door and off the porch, he was greeted by his four demons, they say to Daven our eyes did not go blind, and our skin did not blister, how could this be? So said Daven one of the demons speaks out, my lord Daven this means Satin has brought fourth change but how said Daven, that is a question that could only be answered by lord Satin, or one of any lead demon. Our job is to protect you at all times even against Satin if we must.

We must return at once to seek the truth of this matter. There is something much more to this as they walked through the field an disappeared back to Satins realm.

Chapter Three: Daven speaks to Satin

Father my Lord Satin how is it the sun rises at night upon mother earth said Daven my son Daven I just upset the balance of time a little no matter what in a few days earth and heaven will be ours to claim. But how said Daven when you my son completed a miracle upon mother earth with my blood with in your body, place me there outside beyond the gray line that separates good from evil day from night and heaven from hell. And by doing so my son it weakened the line, so I and my army of demons may cross over and plague mother earth.

This act will bring fourth a great war between heaven and hell and settle all differences between the two. By bringing a large army of demon in great number it will upset the balance between good and evil. By evil out weighing the good. We can control the heaven and all that comes with it said Satin. But what about men kind. There would be some causalities and changes like in all acts of war. But at lease you would have your revenge against God. For act he played against you.

Father my lord, Satin when will I know it's time. When earths midday sunburn a fiery red and hells darkness creeps upon the land. That is when the invasion of mother earth begins son.

Daven then felt with in his heart that he must warn his family upon mother earth. About the Great War. For his love for them was also greater then that of war. So Daven knew that he must return to mother earth. TO inform his brother John about Satin's plot and the day to come. Daven then summon his four demons but only three respond. So he searched the cave inside Satin realm looking for his fourth demon. Daven comes upon a stream that is deserted. My lord Daven the demon said do you search for me. Yes-said Daven.

As Daven got closer to the stream he started to feel ill. So he asked what is this place. This stream of liquid that flows comes from all of these demons around us. For this stream that flows it is of our urine. It is not pleasant to smell. The smell drives demons insane causing them to turn against one another. For the black stallion we ride one drop of it. Make them buck and kill their riders. If the hound of hell should sniff it. He would turn against his master demon and maul him to death. For this urine itself is also wicked and evil, then all the demon combined. So let's move away for here at once. Daven returned to mother earth with his four demons and informs his brother John about Satin's plot. An day's to come. Yet lurking in the shadow is Satin lead demon. He feels that Daven spends too much time with the humans. And less time on plotting the war to come. With Satin permission he cursed Daven with a spell of forget fullness.

As John speaks to Daven he started to feel disoriented, dazed and then stunned like a deer who has ran in front of the head lights of a car. He tried to focus himself. And Gathered up all his thoughts In front of his brother John, Daven eyes changed from the soft brown in to a fiery red. What's wrong Daven? Asked John. Go away for I have been cursed Daven fight to hold on to his memories. He summon his for demon to come into the house my lord Daven what is wrong? Find the demon. Who has cursed me and bring him forth, now go! Yes my lord.

The four demons disappeared in front of John eyes. And return just as fast with a beaten battered beast, within their grasp kneel him down said Daven do you know the punishment for the curse you plagued upon me? I don't have to answer you Daven I can only be tried by lord Satin. Why do you bother with these humans any way, for they all will be dead by tomorrow? There are two ways to remove a curse demon, one if you do it freely or two by death. To hell with you Daven!

Daven stood to his feet and shoved his hand down the throat of Satins lead demon and pulled his cold black heart out.

His mind was at ease again, my lord Daven what should we do with the body? We will return it to Satin. Why we don't serve Satin we only serve you, our job is to protect you and you did very well said Daven. We will take it back, my brother John.,Daven said I have a plan that would protect your family, and mankind from the war to come. So Daven and his four demons return to the stream of urine in which he threw the lead demons body and heart in. he covered his nose with a cloth and held his breathe, and then filled jugs after jugs of the liquid substance. He then sealed it tight, carefully so he would not spill not one drop. Then he returned to earth with his four demons.

Chapter Four: Daven Speaks To John

John tells every man, women, and child to board up their homes and barns and take shelter in the basement. Bring plenty of food and water, and do the same for the animals, in these mugs is a liquid that will protect you pour it around your home, your barn, and around the outside of your cellar. Give it to your friends and anyone that will except it for when the demons of hell rain upon this land, those who walk upon mother earth will be enslaved, or imprisoned the women and their daughters will be raped, and the men and their sons will be murdered. The first-born son will be sacrificed on to your lord God to shame him for deserting man. You must deliver the message and liquid to the people as soon as possible, John make them listen start with the churches, and spread the message like butter on toast. So Daven and his demons returned to Satins underworld to stall the war giving John enough time to inform the people of mother earth about Satins plot. And to gather more jugs from the stream of urine to protect them,

At this time Mother Nature and father time appears in heaven my lord God said Mother Nature, there is a big change upon mother earth, so big that I cannot control it. My lord God may I speak said father time, there has been a large tear in time, were days have become nights, and nights have become days. Minutes hours, months and years will soon fly by so fast that a child born today will be an adult by tomorrow. God sat back in his chair and thinks to himself, how could this be, then God called to his angels, go to Atlantic on mother earth and check the place were we imprisoned the child called Daven. For I feel Satin may have betrayed us.

So the angels took flight to mother earth in search of the place were God has laid Daven to rest. They find the burial place to be empty, so the angels fly back in to the heavens, my lord God the child is gone we looked in on him as you asked, not even his coffin remains. God speaks Satin has tricked us all into capturing the child, for him for he could not do it by himself, what a web we weave and for what purposes. What wicked little scheme is Satin up to? Fly back to mother earth to the farm that the child Daven loves so much, for he has family there, stay far out of sight but watch them closely. For the child has a special gift and you may not make it back, so go now and find out the answers that I need to know, said God. So than angels take flight again heading for the one place Daven would return to, a place he called home.

It was not long for the angels to spot Daven for he and his four demons appeared in the field with jugs filled with a liquid substance. They had friends of John and Stevo working along side of them, the men of the cloth and doctors and such came with trucks after trucks, loading and delivering liquid substance. The places they could not reach by truck, Daven and his four demons would take flight,

Daven and one demon head north for the other three one would go south, another east, and the last west. And meet back at the farm. As Gods angels fly back to the heaven only one stays behind to find out more about what was going on, as one of Davens demon return to the farm to gather more jugs, he spots Gods angel who has stayed behind, as the angel creeps to the back of the barn were they keep the jugs of urine, Davens demon bounced upon it and held it down so it could not fly away.

Face to face they meet the demon finds the angel to be beautiful she was perfect in every way, so he summoned Daven and the three demons to return. There is a spy among us lord Daven, said his demon it is an angel of God, what should we do with it? He replied, Daven another demon said, we cannot let this angel go, for it will summon God to speak to Satin, and Satin would know of our plans that is true said Daven but my fight is not with the angel nor is it with man kind, people believe in angels maybe she can help us and still keep her faith and promise to God, so she wont be damned. Let me speak to her said Daven,

Angel of God these are trouble times for man kind, promise me to keep this secret from God and help us to deliver man kind from evil, said Daven the angel speaks but you are demons your selves, why should I trust you, when Satin is your lord. Then the four demons speak to the angel, this is our lord Daven and we serve only him, not Satin. For Daven he is the reason why we help mankind to prepare for the days to come, it is very rude of you to doubt our lord. With your help we can save more.

Then the angel said if I do not report the truth to God, I will be cursed as being a demon, and then damned from heaven, just tell him you need more time to find the truth, for we did not tell what the days to come will bring. Do not harm the angel said Daven let her be sometime the angel you have makes her decision to be justified in your lords, eyes. Leave us now for we have plenty of work to do, so the angel took to the heavens and returned to the heaven and gave her report, on her findings, my lord God the child has his own gate way, he appeared in the field of the farm with jugs of liquid substance that they had loaded upon trucks to deliver they handed it out to the people of mother earth only to those who except it. The child has four demons that travel north, south, west and east, all across the globe people of earth are boarding up their homes and churches, like if they were preparing for something to come. My lord God may I return to mother earth and meet with the child called Daven? Do you feel you need so my child or should I just inform Satin? Let me be the judge to find the truth, for Satin will hide behind his lies, but for the child there would be some truth in his words.

Send me back with several angels so they may listen to his story as well. So you have spoken to him? Yes my lord. Do you feel you can trust him, either way my lord God do I have a choice? Take the several angels and you may go. Thanks my lord. So the angels headed back to mother earth to meet with the child called Daven.to find the truth that God so needed to seek.

As Daven returned to Satins underworld, Satin summoned Daven to his chambers, my father lord Satin what is it? My son Daven said Satin, it is time to prepare for war you must lead my army of demons across the gray line, into mother earth for I cannot find one of my lead demons, to do so. Have you seen yes my lord upon mother earth, he had plagued me with the disease of forgetfulness, and what did you do with him? I reached down his throat and pulled his heart out, and placed his body and heart in the stream of urine. For disrespecting me.

Daven could you please remove him from that awful place and place the body in hells fire to be burned., before the corpse rots, and stinks up the whole place. Yes father but before I go did you send him to do harm to me? My son Daven, no. He did it out of his own free will, and has been punished for it. For sometimes I seen him getting more jealous of you as your father I should have kept the peace, and for this I have betrayed you, both. Now go and remove his body from the stream and prepare yourself for war. Yes my lord.

After Daven has done all he needed to do Satin then for bided him to return to earth, they feed into his mind all the wickedness of evil and hate, in a room filled with demons, Satin would not know if one was missing, for Satin was only focused on Daven, The demon returns back to the farm and speaks to lord Daven, brother John my lord cannot return back to earth, until the day of the war. He sends a message you must be in your shelters at midday when the sun burns a fiery red. At the base of your homes, barns, stores, and churches pour the liquid I have given you, around them. Do not come out at any time until I come for you. For death wont be swift, it will be painful, and linger like the ringing in your ears, as the demon gets ready to leave he is then bounced on by the angel that lord Daven set free. Were the child called Daven? IT doesn't matter help these people to deliver the liquid so you can take flight in to the heavens before mother earths sun burns a fiery red. Why said the angel, there is no time for why. I must go now there are several of us we can question him more, let him be said the angel, and lets do what he has asked of us. For the answer is here.

We just have to find the right one to ask, than angel sees John are you the brother of the one called Daven? Yes I am, said John what are all these people doing here? They are delivering the liquid to protect us from Satins demons, how could that be said the angel Satin has found a way to cross over the gray line, by this time tomorrow the war to end all wars, will begin. The angel speaks to the other, we must finish what the child Daven started you three return to heaven and speak to our lord, God with some disturbing news, about Satins plan, of war and how the child advised mankind to protect his self against it. Alert the angels and the saints to me in the kingdom hall at once. Said God. And find my son Jesus, yes my lord.

Chapter Five: God summons, mother Nature, Father Time, and the Grim reaper

God speaks to his congregation some how Satin has freed the child, from his coffin and removed the curse we have plagued upon him, it was Satin who has tricked us all, into believing what he wanted us to believe, so he can claim the child as his own. So what is the little devil up to now? Said Father time. He has a plan it has something to do with that child, so keep your eyes open and your ears, and nose to the grindstone. For Satin is up to something.

And the child is the key, said God. One of Gods angels speaks out, my lord we should put a force of angels upon mother earth, to protect mankind, just in case what the child has done for them is not enough. My lord may I speak, said one of the saints, if the child is working with Satin, why does he care what happens to mankind? God speaks, the child is not at war with mankind, nor is it with the angels, but with your lord God himself, for Satin has filled his heart with such grief and his mind with lies. So he can not see the truth but hear only the words of Satin, ok said God we will send down a force of angels as a defense while my son Jesus and I prepare an unbeatable army to defeat Satin and his demons,

Descend the angels at once to mother earth. But keep me informed of any strange happenings. Yes my lord, hidden by my clouds I will keep my eyes open upon the gray line, to see what becomes of it. Said Mother Nature. So be it said God everything is in order now. So you may be dismissed. As Gods angels departed back at Satins under world they prepare for a coming out feast, for the demons of war. As the wine is poured Satin secretly slit his wrist and filled a cup with his blood. He then blessed the cup to cool it so it would quench the thirst of who ever drink it.

Daven sit down next to lord satin, he offers him the cup drink a toast with your father, my son. For the heaven and earth and all that come with it will soon be at our mercy, to lord Satin the greatest ruler of all times, now drink. Daven felt ill as Satins blood filled his belly, like a poison it raced through his vain causing his heart to beat faster, the blood of Satin formed new blood cells that strengthened Daven, his face and body features changed into a beast like a demon.

Daven who Satin now calls lord Daven Satins demon warlord. All but Davens four demons cheered for him, what has Satin done to our lord Daven. One of Satins demons speaks to them, he has been cursed by the blood of Satin, for the time of war is near, midday tomorrow we ride upon mother earth to raise hell, and to begin the apocalypse. In the morning the demons get ready to plague their assault upon mother earth and take the fight onto the heavens. Daven mounts on to his horse with authority, as midday approaches on mother earth, the sun changes from bright yellow to a fire ball red, the army of demons leave hell marching toward the gray line, heading for mother earth with war lord Daven leading the way.

Chapter Six: The Arch Diocese Speaks

The prophecy in which the child Daven spoke about is upon us snow, inform the people to run and hide, for death will be in thy name. We are living in our last days brother an disasters, for the child named Daven has sided with Satin, this news traveled from town to town over mountains, through out the valley in and about the big city. From land to land, it sent panic all over mother earth, reverends, and pastors, preachers, cardinals, and bishops carried the news to the pope. This child called Daven spoke of a war evil verse good, and it is upon us today. The pope speaks yes I remember the child called Daven, several years ago we asked for a miracle from him, instead of a miracle he spared us our lives we should have been thankful, instead of banishing him we should have brought him closer to God. By speaking to him instead of at him. And maybe we would not be in this predicament; we are in today.

Bring me Reverend Paul of the eastern monastery now for timing is of the essence. For reverend Paul is a good friend of the one called Daven, we would speak to Daven in our behalf to seek the truth about this war, but our Pontiff we may be to late then it is in the hand of our lord God. Yet we must try anyway, and have faith in Reverend Paul. We will leave at once, as midday arrived hells darkness creeps upon the land, the time has begun. They return with Reverend Paul my pontiff you wish to speak to me, said Reverend Paul? Yes I wish for you to speak to the one called Daven to see if we can bring an end to this war. I have not seen or spoke to him in some time, he may not remember me. He has brothers, one is John, and the other is Stevo, I know of them from the letter he read, they live in the farm community. I would start there to see if he shows up. Then I would speak to him, take reverend Paul and reverend Kevin, with you, be safe and may God be with you. Thank you my pontiff so the three head out toward the farm country, to seek Daven and to end the war.

The three reverends reach the family storing plenty of food and fresh water, in the outside cellar, and lowering the children and father Joe down into it. Good afternoon Iam reverend Paul from the eastern monastery, I would like to speak to John or Stevo, the brother of Daven yes I am John and I am Stevo, we are looking for your brother Daven we were sent by the Archdioceses to speak in their behalf, to see if we can end this war. My brothers and I including Davens four demons then by the help of Gods angel have been spreading the word for this day that is coming, it is hard for us to hear through the walls of our monastery, said reverend Paul. Sometimes we are blind and deaf, to the ways of man.

Reverend Paul look around you, for Satins darkness from hell is upon us. Now you should take shelter, it is my word as a reverend to speak to your brother and my good friend Daven. Take these jugs of liquid with you if you get trapped inside of hells darkness bathe yourselves with it, for it will protect you from Satins demons, said John. Pour it around the monastery, and around the Archdioceses, board up the windows, and lock the doors, so the demons cannot get in. so they return to the monastery with jugs of liquid, and inform the director of the monastery what to do. But he was being stubborn, this is holy ground no demon can walk upon this land, when hells darkness close its fist upon mother earth, there will be nothing left to be holy, said reverend Carl, that is the truth said reverend Kevin.

Reverend Paul took some of the jugs to the Archdioceses, and informed them what to do; we will take charge here and do what we need to do. Hurry reverend Paul leave for the Archdioceses, as he looks in to the darkness he can hear the cries of misery, and suffering ring out from the darkness that covered the land. For in the darkness was mans worse nightmare, a horror describable, for men, women, and child. Were tortured, and enslaved, and murdered. the female women, and child was raped, by the demons for they carried the seeds to create life in Satins image. For the men and his first born son, the man was asked, to render their soul on to Satin and to denounce Jesus Christ, and God as their lord. When they refused their first-born son was sacrificed, to shame their lord God for deserting man.

Then the man himself, was tortured, and nailed to an upside down crucifix, then branded on his forehead with the star of Satin. Then left on the side of the road tortured yet still alive, to rot. Those who render their soul were in prisoned, for they lost their faith in God. And to pledge Satin was the only way out leaving men at his wit's end for life, meant more to him then death. Even though he denounced his faith in God, he still lives. As hells darkness creeps slowly further in land it generates its wicked evil ways, among the people in the streets, looting, violence, murder and such bad happens.

Chapter Seven

As reverend Paul reaches the Archdioceses he quickly runs inside, these streets should have been deserted and yet there are people running every were, said reverend Paul. The POPE speaks to reverend Paul, my son have you found the one called Daven? No my pontiff but he has left a liquid, that would repel the demons and keep men from being harmed. We must board up the windows, and lock all the doors, before darkness reaches here. We must act quickly, so they started to board up the windows, and lock the doors, and on the outside, at the base of the building they poured the liquid. From the back to the front, they soaked the boards on the windows and doors. With it.

Then they return inside at this time a hard knock appears at the front door, it is the monastery director, from the eastern monastery, what are you doing here? Said reverend Paul, I did not listen so I left only to see the demons of hell ride into town, they raided each and every house, on the block, dragging out the whole family, kicking and screaming then they question the man of the house. They force him to kneel to the rider, on the horse if he shook his head no, he was tortured and each family member had to watch, as one by one of his family had their head severed off, in front of him to add salt to the wound. They nailed the father to an upside down crucifix; with a hot iron poker they branded a symbol upon his forehead.

As a man of God I could not bear to watch anymore, it was horrible, and heart wrecking. It made me lose my faith for I could not save them. For what he had witnessed made him break down in tears, they are not to far behind me, and it's the child called Daven, who leads them. Then I will go and talk to him, said reverend Paul, that would be suicide said the director, but we must try to end this war said the pope. By any means necessary, as the army of demons moves closer, to the Archdiocese hundreds of men, women, and children bang on the big door, that keeps them locked out. Begging to come in, those are our people out there open the door and let them in. it is to late for them now for if we open those doors we will fall upon deaths door as well. Listen not to their cries for it will be over soon, pray for our lord God to save them.

Yet reverend Paul did not listen to the Archdioceses, rules and ran to the rear of the building and opened the rear doors, he then gathered up as many of the men, women and children he could. Trying to flee from hells destruction, he leads them to the rear doors to the inside of the hall and bolted the door shut. He said, when I knock three times then reopen the doors for I will have others that would need shelter. At this time reverend Paul remembers to bathe himself with the liquid that's inside of the car, then he fills empty bottles with the liquid to baptize men, women, and children with it and the rest as a weapon to clear his way back to the Archdiocese, as reverend Paul use the liquid he noticed that the hounds of hell, and the black stallion they walk with, and ride upon turn against their riders and masters, and the demons against each other. For today reverend Paul was mans savior, for his bravery later on he would become a saint. As reverend Paul single handedly fought the odd forces, of evil. He finally meets up with Daven, or someone of a beast like Daven, how do you see man? Asked reverend Paul, I see man as a lost lamb, among the wolves said warlord Daven. Is that the reason why you hunt them like wild game, said reverend Paul?

Man has lost himself in many ways, reverend Paul. In social and economic. The life style between the rich and poor, not only do they pollute the air, but they're self with drugs, to escape reality. They take the life of their unborn, by abortion. And then there is pedophilia, oh my said lord Daven. Reverend Paul said Daven; we cannot blame ourselves for what wrong man has done in their lives. We can only pray for them, and hope things will get better. Man is a disease that plague mother earth, and that's why God has turned his back on him, man will destroy man and then turn on himself, said war lord Daven. For it is his doing, it is his way, it is his life. That is why when one war ends another war begins, for man cannot live with each other, nor himself, and death would be his last reward. For this war would end all wars, any differences that mankind may have, thanks to his sins.

Now kneel before me reverend Paul, do you except Satin as your one true God? What has become of you my son, were is that caring, loving person that I use to know, so well gone? War lord Daven then dismounted from his horse and lifted reverend Paul off his feet, by the neck and said to hell I went then snapped his neck, killing him. Daven looked into the lifeless eyes of a friend, and inside of both of his hearts, something happened to him. For he has never killed such a holy man before, in his heart it felt like if he had never betrayed any one he loved before, and this laid heavy on his demon soul. No matter how hard he tried to use his gift he could not bring reverend Paul back, he could not for Satins blood would not let him, for it controlled him now and his gift as well.

Hurt by the death of his good friend, cursed by the blood of Satin, Daven then looked among the ruins, and sees the lives he had part in taking. What have I become, he said to himself, for my fight is not with men, but with God himself.

Chapter Eight

As Daven kneel by the body of his good friend, he forced out the wicked blood of Satin, through the pores of his skin. At this time his four demons arrive my lord Daven, the angels of God are here, to push the demons of Satin back in to hell. What has cursed you with his blood? My lord. The angels start with there attack against the evil of Satin. The angels remove the body of reverend Paul, and carry it up to the heavens, before the demons have the chance to desecrate it. As the angels approach Daven and his four demons Satins lead demon rides upon them, lord Daven, get to your feet, and mount your horse. Soon the Son of God will be upon us. You are the Prentiss of lord Satin so why do you weep for men?

As the angels and demons, fight around him lord Daven rises to his feet and mounts his horse once again. With his four demons to protect him he rides off. One of the four demons notice the blood, my lord Daven you bleed do not worry for it is not my blood. But the blood of satin, it is the way he keeps mans mind imprisoned by poisoning the blood of his wicked ways. Then feed his mind with evil thoughts, and doings. It is he who helps men to loss his way and become lost in his or her world of sins for he will temp man with temptations and temptation will always be there for man. It is like that beautiful man or woman that a wife or husband, would remove their wedding bands, breaking the vows that they made to each other and to God.

To make disappear the faith and trust they had found in one another leaving the family in ruins, and shame, for secrets never die, and forgiveness is sometimes hard to find in one self, and anger and hate play the part of being disappointed not with your mate but with yourself. Called guilt for that's how I feel today guilty for being productive in doing Satins sins. With some of the blood of Satin out of his system, he could think clearly so he put an end to the slaughtering and rape of innocent people. For those demons, which didn't obey his words, were put to death by his hands. This did not go well with the second demon of command, so he returns to speak with Satin, my lord Satin, the child has rejected your blood it flows from the skin of his pores, like sweat. He has put a stop to the enslaving, torture, and murder of men. Forbidding of any raping, of women, or child.

If we do not obey his words we are put to death. And some of man has the stream of urine to protect them. Does Daven still fight against God? He does, the fight is still against God, said Satin. Yet he weeps for man, keep a close eye on him. Let me know of any more changes in his behavior, for this can be a problem on controlling mother earth and the heavens. Inform the demons to obey Davens laws, for we can spawn later and have man render his soul unto me. Now go said Satin. The army obeys Satins ruling and imprisoned men, women, and children inside a mountain of rocks. As the war progresses through the days and nights, and the months turn out to be years, Satin was satisfied. The power of Daven and the rage he had inside of him plowed through the angels like a bowling ball does pins. But three angels were relentless they would come back stronger, and in greater numbers to change the balance of good over evil.

So Daven then formed a miracle and impregnated all the female women, and children with the spirits of the angels. This decreased the angels in great numbers and it weakened their defense. And this angered Satin, for now he could not bare a child in his image.

Chapter Nine: Satin Summons Lord Daven

My son Daven you have seized on torturing and killing man, you have forbid my army of demons to rape, and to create life in my image. Now you have impregnated all the women, and children with the spirits of angels. My lord Satin you are truly in a dilemma were a father who denies his child, that is his, and a father who believes the child that is his, but is not. When you become ruler, of both heaven, and hell you may choose any form you want. For all would be your children, but for I would still be Daven.

A demon comes and interrupts them, lord Satin, Lord Daven, you must return to mother earth, at once for a new threat is upon us. As Jesus, his saints, and Gods best eight angels, descend from the heavens upon mother earth, Jesus summons for mother nature who hides behind the clouds, to join them on the battle field, for her strength was also needed. Jesus asked of his saints and eight angels, to find the child and keep a close eye on him. For he is the key of Satins powers, and strength, that is released upon mother earth.

If we capture the child Jesus said, it would weaken Satins army, then we can push them back to hell from which they came and seal the gray line forbidding this from happening again. Yet be careful, for the child Daven has a gift like all of us. Though he weakens and must sleep from time to time, after performing to many miracles this would be our opportunity to seize the child, and imprison him within the heavens, as our lord God has planned.

Then Jesus asked of Saint Joseph to heal those who are ill and near death, and for Grim Reaper to bless the dead and return their soul onto their father God. He asked of Moses to free those who are imprisoned and enslaved, then asked of him to take them some where safe, with mankind out of reach and safe from harm Jesus then set up his battle field like a game of chess. With lord Jesus as the king Mother Nature as the queen, Moses with his mighty staff and Grim Reaper with his mighty sickle, as his knight with Saint Joseph, and Saint Peter, as his bishops. And for his rooks, were Saint Anthony, and Saint Jude, with Gods best of eight angels as his pawns.

They said a small blessing; bless on to me lord God, of Abraham, the strength and courage we need to succeed. In Jesus name Amen. Then they went to war. As Daven returns to mother earth from Satins under world, he mounts his horse and gives his final speech to Satins army of demons. This is the moment we have been waiting for, to fight with Gods best of the best, and push them back into the heavens, were our lord Satin will become God, and I lord Daven his son to rule for all eternity,

As lord Daven gives Satins demons the order to charge. Jesus army waits patiently, as the demons approach, the eight angels pawns move forward, they spread their wings and begin to flap, while doing so they release hollow point feathers, that fly into the demons of hell paralyzing them, then the angels remove their halos and cut there way through Satins defense moving Jesus army also closer. As more angels fly down from the heavens to intervene with the fight, Mother Nature moves forward and summons the hurricane gale winds, to plow the demons back across the gray line.

As Daven and Satins army of demons regroup Daven then summons, up a storm of his own a big tornado rips across the battlefield, then he summons bolts of lightning striking down his adversaries. He gives Satins demons a second command to charge forward, Moses, and Grim Reaper, take their place upon the battle field, with each at separate ends, they both hammer the ground with their mighty staff, and sickle, causing the earth to open.

As Daven and Satin lead demon gives their order for the demons of hell to charge forward, they fall in to the great big gap, trapping their selves inside of the belly of mother earth. As the great big gap closes, Jesus army then charges forward with new angels that seem to rain down from the heavens, to replace the angels that have fallen. Feeling out numbered, they send a demon back to ask Satin for more reinforcements, to push Jesus army back, doing so Satin sacrificed men with great sins upon their soul. And by doing so he weakened Daven from his gift, of power, for it is mans sin that kept him strong, as Daven falls to his knees the four saints quickly surround him, forbidding the sins of man to get through to strengthen him, the angels then quickly surround the four saints, making a strong unbreakable barrier. Keeping Davens four demons that protect him, at bay, and Satins army from retrieving the child.

Jesus then summoned God to raise Daven up into the heavens, to in prison him from the war. As Daven weakens he becomes very ill with a fever, he pukes blood from his inner body that stains the heavens. God is not pleased with this for it is some kind of infection that would plague the heavens, so God summoned for Jesus. Jesus then looked upon Daven and said to God, it is the blood of Satin he has poisoned the child with it so he may control him. Jesus then speaks to Daven;

eat of this bread, for it is of my body, drink this wine from thou cup for it is my blood. The blood and the body of Christ freed lord Daven, from the spell of Satin, and restored him back into the spirit he use to be, as the word of Daven being captured rang out among the heavens, the word did not go so well in hell, for Satin was beside himself,

He speaks to his lead demon; did he surrender his soul on to God? Begging for forgiveness like a dog does for a bone? No my lord, then how asked Satin, did he get captured? My lord Satin, when you sacrificed the men that had many sins, against him you weakened lord Daven. We must get him back; it's far to late for that for God has imprisoned him in the heavens. Then I must take command upon mother earth, and push the fight up into the heavens, and free my son lord Daven. Tell the army of demons to regroup while I summon hell upon earth, now go.

As mother earth suddenly changes to hell, suitable for Satin to walk upon, the angels stand in fright as the beast arrives. Hells darkness completely covers mother earth. And it affects mankind in the worse way, it brings forth sin in man makes him wicked and evil, the world that God tried so hard to save becomes and the people that Moses freed, and Saint Joseph healed, all run a muck upon mother earth. With their looting, and rioting, violence, murder and rapes. The dead walks among the demons to help make Satins army stronger.

Back in heaven Daven is surrounded by the four saints at all times as he waits four visitors pay him a visit, it is the spirit of his mother Heidi, his brother David, and his wife Doris, along with saint Paul, they came to speak to Daven. My son, Daven why is your heart filled with so much pain, and grief? Said Heidi. Mother Heidi it was you who taught love, kindness, and respect. Your death is the reason why my heart cries. For the lose of your love, silly child my love for you has never died, it remains in your heart, as well as in mine.

You must find peace with in your self, Daven. But mother my love for my brother and his wife were taken while I was away, I could have saved them and brought them back and now there's shame upon my heart. For the loss of their lives. Then the reverend Paul a good friend that I betrayed and put to death by my hands, it brought sorrow upon my heart and soul. How can I seek forgiveness in the eyes of God, when the ones I need to hear it from are here in heaven? I tried seeking God to learn all of his wisdom, but was turned away the man of the cloth.

Satin opened his heart to me, filled the empty spaces in my heart, for his love is all I know. As Daven speaks to his family, and dear friend Jesus listens and decides that Daven is a good child, that just lost his way, and in Jesuses heart he felt sorrow, for Satin took advantage of poor Daven while he was grieving, and mourning the death of his loved ones. And turned him into his wicked, evil ways. It was Satin said Daven, who fed my mind with lies, he led me to believe that God was the reason for the death of all that stand before me, then imprisoned me so I could not seek the truth.

Brother Daven said Saint Paul, forgiveness starts when you can forgive your self, then others come to forgive you. Yes Daven that is true said David. Then Doris speaks Daven you have the most warm, caring heart, then any man alive when I was a demon in love you did not cast me out of your family, yet you blessed me with a soul of my own, and Iam very thankful to you. Then why do I feel so alone said Daven? You are not alone said David; our family upon mother earth needs you more than ever now, if they are to survive. Yes said Heidi for you Daven will always be part of our family. In time Daven I know you will make everything right.

Chapter Ten: The Trial Of Daven

Daven is brought in to be tried by God for his disobedience upon mother earth, and his acts against God. Jesus speaks on Davens behalf, before the trial begins father said Jesus, who are we to judge the child Daven, when it is us who has failed him? If this is so my son Jesus then prove it to me. I shall said Jesus let me speak to him alone. That would be wise of you said God, for his powers are equal to mine not of yours. Then to seek the truth is a risk that I must take, said Jesus. So be it said God. So Jesus speaks to Daven, Daven tell me all about yourself, so I may represent you in the eyes of God.

So Daven told Jesus from the beginning to now, you are truly a child who has lost his way, said Jesus but it is the man of the cloth who has kept you from seeking God. And yet it was Satin who has preyed upon you, to bring fourth this act of war, of sac religion, to claim heaven and earth as his own. It is Satin who should be on trial, not you Daven. Out of all you have been through there is still an ounce of good left in you? And father will hear the truth.

As the trial begins the spirit of Heidi speaks to God, my son not from my womb, but from my heart, have mercy on him for he has been influenced by Satin, and has lost his way. Give him a chance to redeem himself in your eyes, so he may find peace with in himself, once again. Very well said God, I will take this into consideration, for the motherly love in you for your son is strong and my son Jesus has grown fond of him.

As Daven is brought before God, to try there is pandemonium in heaven, angels speak out against Daven, all at once, disgrace him fill his heart with great pain, and sorrow. Then tears fall from his eyes, for he knows that it would be hard to find forgiveness, for the crimes that he has taken part of. And it echoes loud and clear among the heavens, so God calls the heaven to order and silences it. Then Jesus spoke, listen to yourselves speaking out against Daven, we to are acting like children who doesn't like the smell of their own stench? From their own body being foul. He is like the child of mother earth, he who did not ask to be born, but yet is. Abused by his peers, hurt by grief, betrayed and imprisoned by the blood of Satin

. Who are we to judge in the eyes of God? There's no repent to Jesus statement, for a fare trial Daven would get. As the charges and Davens defense go back and fourth, it is interrupted, an angel appears in heavens court room, my lord

God I wish to speak to you, in private, it is important that I do. So God takes a ten-minute recess. What is so important said God? It is Satin said the angel he is upon mother earth, he seeks the child. He has taken the wings off the backs of the fallen angels and placed them on the backs of his demons, to take flight, he said if the child is not returned back to him at once he will bring the fight into the heavens. To free the child and become God. Is that so said God?

That is so, said the angel. Then I shall go and speak with Satin, court is adjourned, said God. Father Jesus what is so important that you must adjourn? it is Satin my son, he is upon mother earth, he has threatened to bring his army of demons to free the child, and to become God. My son Jesus keep an eye on the child, for if I fail Satins demons will take him for sure. So God set out to mother earth, to rid the world of Satin, and his vermin demons, that plagues upon her.

Chapter Eleven: God Speaks To Satin

Return to your underworld and free mankind, and mother earth from your grasp said God. Return my son Daven to me said Satin, or my demons will rain upon the heaven and I will become God. God was at his wits end with Satin, to fight him and his demons. God remembers the gift that Daven gave to man, to ward off the demons, so God went to Satins underworld to find the stream of urine that flows. God then evaporated the liquid and changed it to a gas that filled the cloud above, mother earth. And then God took a single star from the heavens, and transformed it into a bright sun, that shined upon mother earth this blinded and blistered the demons and cast out hells darkness that plagued upon mother earth.

God then released the gas of urine from the clouds in the form of rain, as this covered Satins demons hounds of hell, and the black stallion in which they rode upon. Turn against one another to fight to the death .God then gives his angels of war the signal, to fly down upon the demons, and to end this war. This did not go well with Satin so out of anger he lashed out at God, and the battle upon mother earth like siblings, do when they cant get their way. There was light and thunder, earthquakes, title waves, and volcano eruptions, if they did not stop the world would be destroyed, and there will be no heaven or hell, nor mother earth to lay their burden upon. To exist would be no more. The fighting pauses for a moment between God and Satin, and God speaks to Satin once again,

Satin why have you risen up against me? For far to long your creation of man in your image, has blamed me for their sins, upon mother earth yet they come to me for forgiveness, and dam my name. I only gave man free will, so he may think for himself, and choose for himself. Yet you set laws, and the rules of the Ten Commandments that   man must follow and obey did man no said Satin; so send your only son Jesus to die for you, by the hands of man. To rid them of there sins only for man to sin again. Your bible reads of me, as a demon like beast with evil and wicked ways and fallen from your good grace. For not obeying your rules together we created, but you took credit for it all, Satin said to God.

What is written is written but God you have forsaken me and replaced me with your own son, so what is the purpose of this war said God. To free myself and to claim my rights as being God said Satin. Your plans of over throughing me has failed the blood and the body of Christ. Casting out all of your evil and wicked ways, Noooo! Screamed Satin he has betrayed me, no said God you have betrayed yourself, for his heart is bigger than yours

Satin then rose to his feet, then the fighting assume again. With Satin refusing to back down and God determined to push him back from which he came. God asked Satin for forgiveness but Satin was being selfish and rude towards God. So God and his mighty strength throw Satin back across the gray line. Only for Satin to rise up more courage able and angry then ever. Satin speaks Jehovah God all mighty give me back my son. The child means a lot to you said God. Yes said Satin with our powers, combined we will defeat you and I will become God. An heaven and hell would be no more. Sins of man will live forever as mankind is created in my image. There would be no difference. No gray line to keep me a prisoner, separated from the rest of the world. The freedom to come and go as I please. Instead of angels being born without sin, Demons will be born with sins upon sins.

And Lord Daven will live upon mother earth as their keeper and a God. You are foolish said God to Satin. The world could not exist with just sin. There has to be balance between good and evil for men or demons to coexist. For every being has an opinion that must be stated and choices and risks that they must take. With out the gray line to separate the balance between good and evil may Hein and anarchy will happen. And the worlds that you have made for your self will one-day rise up against you said God.

That's why said Satin, I need my son Daven. To keep order among them all, so bring me my; child.   It was too dangerous for the Angels or demons only Jesus himself could intervene and separate the two. The fighting has become critical the more Satin rises up. The more determined God became to drive him back. The Angel's and demons has long ended the fight for their greatest fear. For mother earth was crumbling beneath their feet. For her core could not take much more of their abuse upon her. She weakens.

Chapter Twelve:

Mother Heidi said Daven I know what I must do to end this war. I must sacrifice my life upon the gray line to strengthen it making it strong once again. This would bring back the balance between good and evil and return Satin back to his proper place. The memories of my existing will be gone forever. Yet you David and Reverend Paul will live again but without Doris, for when I die my creation dies to. Just keep an eye on Stevo for his death was an accident with in the barn. And will repeat it self after I am gone. Joe will see again but, in his heart he would never touch another drink. Betty and John will meet again later in life. And Betty will bear him two boys. Peace will come to mother earth. For the sins of men will die with me my son Daven said Heidi. Is this the only way? Yes said Daven. It would set everything back in it's right order if choose not to exist.

Heidi and Daven spook with Jesus about his plans and Jesus agreed. For mother earth and mankind would be no more and to Jesus both creations were worth saving. Daven then said his good byes, hugged his mother Heidi, and then kisses her. Then with in a blink of an eye he was gone. As a streak of life flies overhead of God and Satin. Satin speaks, it is my son Daven my faith lies, with in him. I shall become God. Jesus said God let him be farther said Jesus for he has made his decision to end this war and bring peace to us all. So be it said God.

As Daven stood upon the gray line, he then slit both of his wrists as his farther did in the past. As his blood flow upon it, it strengthens the gray line and the world that rotated clockwise paused for a moment then rotated counter clockwise. This reverse action causes time to change from the presence back into the past. A great vacuum suction affect happen upon mother earth. It pulled Satin and his army of demons back across the gray line and imprison him back in hell. It restored the damage that was done upon mother earth and to man as will. It brings back life from death. It also erases the minds of man. Those who came to know and to love Daven has forgotten him completely and of the war that has occurred. Except for on person, his mother Heidi. For in her heart, soul and mind she waited for him to be reborn.

As the gray line opens once again like a woman's womb. Daven then falls inside. He finds himself at peace. As he slits his wrist it closes and heals, the gray line changes into a band of silver. It glows as Daven sleep's, he changes from that of a young man into that of a little boy in to the state of a baby then that of a fetus. Then back into the seed from which he came.

It has been ten years and all has been forgotten and erased from men's mind. And just like Daven promised, peace has come to mother earth for the sins of man have died with him. Yet back on the farm life was troublesome. My wife Heidi the farm is in great trouble. I know Joe Heidi said. I pray to God each day for rain. It's the mountains said Joe. It keeps the cloud of rain all to it's self. And just gives us a little shower only enough for the flowers to grow but not for our crops. Be patient my love. God will answer my prayers. In Jesus name Amen, Amen said Joe.

That night the climate changed and rain poured upon the farm. The crops grew in full bloom. A stranger appears in the field he has blessed the farm grounds. Then mount himself upon a horse name Pegasus takes off to the heavens. Yet in the silence of darkness, it was the stranger being watched by a child like figure hiding in the field of corn.